WEST CHICAGO PUBLIC LIBRARY DISTRICT

3 6653 00281 9047

11/19

West Chicago Public Library District
118 West Washington
West Chicago, IL 60185-2803
Phone # (630) 231-1552
Fax # (630) 231-1709

D1265435

BIPOLAR BEAR

Victoria M. Remmel

4880 Lower Valley Road, Atglen, PA 19310

**To my Sun and my Moon and all the Stars in our universe.
May you always know you're loved.**

Copyright © 2019 by Victoria M. Remmel

Library of Congress Control Number: 2019936477

All rights reserved. No part of this work may be reproduced or used in any form or by any means—graphic, electronic, or mechanical, including photocopying or information storage and retrieval systems—without written permission from the publisher.

The scanning, uploading, and distribution of this book or any part thereof via the Internet or any other means without the permission of the publisher is illegal and punishable by law. Please purchase only authorized editions and do not participate in or encourage the electronic piracy of copyrighted materials.

"Schiffer Kids" is a registered trademark of Schiffer Publishing, Ltd.
"Schiffer Kids" logo is a registered trademark of Schiffer Publishing, Ltd.

Edited by Kim Grandizio
Type set in Futura

ISBN: 978-0-7643-5805-0 (hard cover)
ISBN: 978-0-7643-5880-7 (soft cover)
Printed in China

Published by Schiffer Kids
An imprint of Schiffer Publishing, Ltd.
4880 Lower Valley Road
Atglen, PA 19310
Phone: (610) 593-1777; Fax: (610) 593-2002
E-mail: Info@schifferbooks.com
Web: www.schifferbooks.com

For our complete selection of fine books on this and related subjects, please visit our website at www.schifferbooks.com. You may also write for a free catalog.

Schiffer Publishing's titles are available at special discounts for bulk purchases for sales promotions or premiums. Special editions, including personalized covers, corporate imprints, and excerpts, can be created in large quantities for special needs. For more information, contact the publisher.

We are always looking for people to write books on new and related subjects. If you have an idea for a book, please contact us at proposals@schifferbooks.com.

This is Polar Bear.

His
family
lives
right
in
the
middle
Of their very own beautiful planet.

It's not too big

and not too little.

Sometimes Polar Bear's on the North Pole
Dancing without a care.

Sometimes he naps on the South Pole.
That's why he's a bi-polar bear.

Polar Bear walks around the planet

Not sure about what he will find.

One thing he does know for certain:

His family is always on his mind.

When Polar Bear's on the North Pole,
He feels on top of the world.

"The sun shines from every corner!"

He says as he dances and twirls.

The
   sun
      rays
         beam
            down
               upon
                  him.

Everything seems **INTENSE** and **BRIGHT.**

"I'm so dizzy from spinning around!"
The sun makes him lose his sight.

Sometimes his family helps him

Put on **sunglasses** so he knows

How to find the path that will take him

To his **home** back down below.

Sometimes he finds the sunglasses
By feeling around **on his own.**

Sometimes he finds them quickly.

Sometimes it's **longer** for him to get home.

Polar Bear visits the South Pole, too,
On the opposite side of the map.

The planet feels **big** and **heavy.**

He gets tired and just wants to *nap.*

The South Pole is cool and quiet.

Not much of the sun shines there.

"It's hard to see all the beauty,"

Yawned the tired, uninspired polar bear.

"Is anyone there? I can't see a thing."

Sometimes it gets dark as night.

Sometimes Polar Bear's family is there

To give him a **nice**, **bright flashlight.**

At times he finds the flashlight

By himself when everything's **blurry.**

Sometimes . . .

it takes . . .

a rather . . .

long time.

Sometimes he finds it in a hurry.

Either way,

North Pole
or
South Pole,

No matter which way Polar Bear roams,

He always goes to where his heart belongs . . .

Polar Bear always finds his way home.

More than just Polar Bear

(some words about bipolar disorder)

Because we don't hear about it often, there's a belief bipolar disorder is rare. However, as of 2016, it was estimated 40 million people around the world were diagnosed with bipolar disorder (ourworldindata.org/mental-health). It is a complicated disorder that varies across the board in severity and can be difficult to recognize. It always helps to find a therapist you trust to establish a treatment plan that works for you.

Learning to talk about it is a huge step in breaking the stigma around mental health. Like exercise and diet for your physical health, a therapist is great to maintain good mental health no matter what your situation.

If you'd like to learn more, check out these following resources for information:

 www.nami.org/learn-more/mental-health-conditions/bipolar-disorder/support

www.apa.org/topics/bipolar/index.aspx

www.nimh.nih.gov/health/topics/bipolar-disorder/index.shtml

These sunglasses and flashlight are meant to represent treatment in all forms. Each person is unique, as is their method for living with bipolar disorder.

These tools can give a voice to loved ones who might otherwise feel helpless.

If someone hands them to you, it's okay to let them know that this is a time when you need to find them on your own.

Cut only with adult supervision

1. Cut page from book.

2. Cut sunglasses along dashed line.

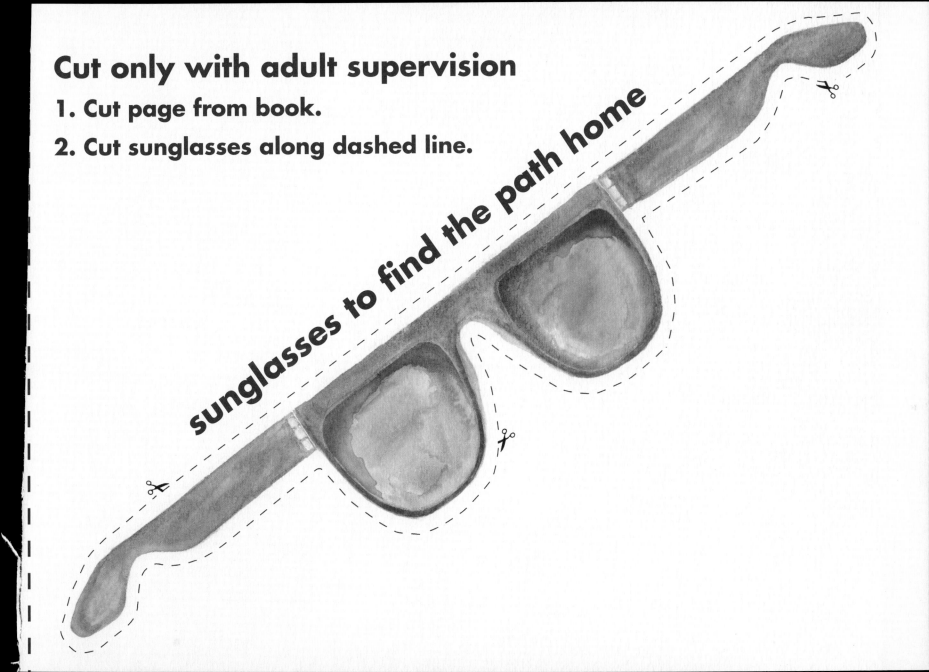

sunglasses to find the path home

Sometimes Polar Bear's family helps him. Sometimes he finds the sunglasses by feeling around on his own.

**POLAR
BEAR
ALWAYS**

**FINDS
HIS WAY
HOME.**

a nice, bright flashlight

Cut only with adult supervision

1. Cut page from book.

2. Cut flashlight along dashed line.

POLAR BEAR ALWAYS FINDS HIS WAY HOME.

Sometimes Polar Bear's family is there.
At times he finds the flashlight by himself.